Unicor[n Stories]
and How to Tell Them
By Rich Linville

ISBN: 9781520144993

Q. Why does a unicorn have only one horn?
A. Because if it had two horns, it would be a cow.

Q. What happens when you put a unicorn and a cow between two slices of bread?
A. You get a corned beef sandwich.

Q. What do you call a single ear of corn?
A. A unicorn.

Q. What did the baby unicorn call her father?
A. "Pop" corn!

Q. What kind of jokes does a unicorn tell?
A. Corn-ey jokes!

Q. Why did the unicorn go to the movies?
A. Because she loved the book so much!

Q. What is the difference between a carrot and a unicorn?
A. One is a bunny feast and the other is a funny beast!

Q. Why did the unicorn join the police force?
A. She wanted to
    wear a uniform!

Q. Why don't unicorns like wearing hats?
A. The hats keep ripping on their horns.

Q. How did the unicorn get a black eye??
A. From an ingrown horn!

Q. What are unicorn dandruff flakes called?
A. Cornflakes!

Q. Why are you like a cat unicorn?
A. Because you're too good to be true!

Q. What did one unicorn say to the other?
A. Your pace is familiar but I can't remember your mane!

Q. What did the Unicorn say to the Zebra?
A. U-No-Corn!

Q. How did the unicorn get a headache?
A. He bumped his horn on a low doorway!

Q. What do you call a unicorn with plastic surgery?
A. A horse.

Q. Why did the horse order ice cream?
A. To put the empty cone on his head and be a unicorn.

Q. What is a Unicorn's favorite ride?

A. A Unicycle!

Q. Are unicorns real?
A. Yes, they're big, gray and called rhinos!

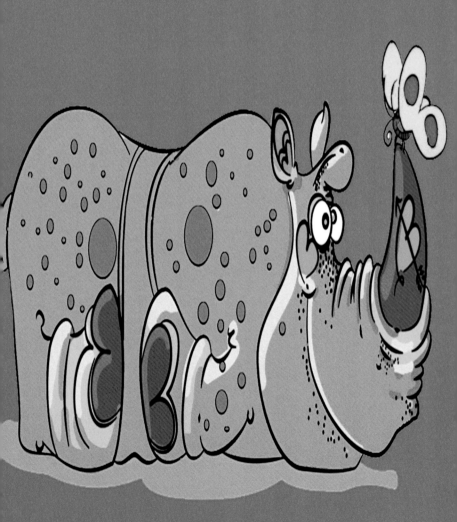

Q. What did the cereal bowl say to the glass of milk with a straw sticking out of it?
A. Ooh! You look just like a unicorn!

Q. What do you do if you see a unicorn?
A. Stop eating junk food. It's making you have delusions!

Q. What game should you never play with unicorns?
A. Leap frog!

- Knock! Knock!
- Who's there?
- Unicorn!
- Unicorn who?
- Unicorn-iest joke teller that I know!

Q. What do you call a
Unicorn's best friend?
A. A corn dog!

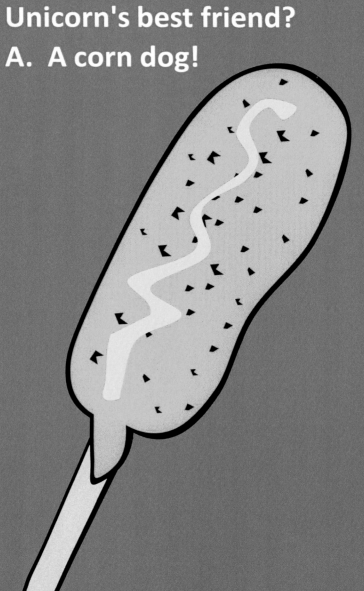

Q. What do you call a Unicorn with 3 Horns?
A. A unique-corn!

Q. What's the best way for keeping calm?
A. By riding a unicorn!

Q. What do you do if your friends say that you're crazy?
A. You get down off of your unicorn and tell them that you're not crazy!

Q: What do you call a unicorn that gets good grades?
A: An "A" corn.

Q: What do unicorns use for money?
A: Corn "Bread".

A child loses her favorite book. A month later, a unicorn walks up to her carrying the book in its mouth. The girl couldn't believe her eyes. She took her favorite book out of the unicorn's mouth. She says, "It's a miracle!" The unicorn replies. "Not really because your name and address is written inside the book cover."

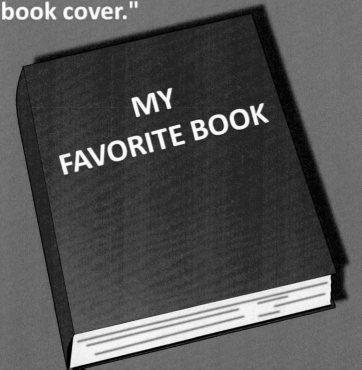

MY FAVORITE BOOK

Q: What did Santa say when he saw a unicorn?
A: Santa said,
"Wow! A unicorn. You're for real."

Q: What did the unicorn say when he ran into the ice cream shop?
A: "Ouch!"

Q: Where did the unicorns play football?
A: In the corn field.

Is laughter really the best medicine?

Scientists have found that laughter can make me healthier and happier. A day without learning and laughing at myself or with others is a day wasted! Be careful not to hurt someone's feelings with a joke.

I am going to buy or check out from the library some humor or joke books. After I find clean jokes that I like, I'll memorize them. I will tell a joke to 10 different people even if they don't laugh or don't get the joke. Now that joke is a part of me and a part of my sense of humor to use in the future!

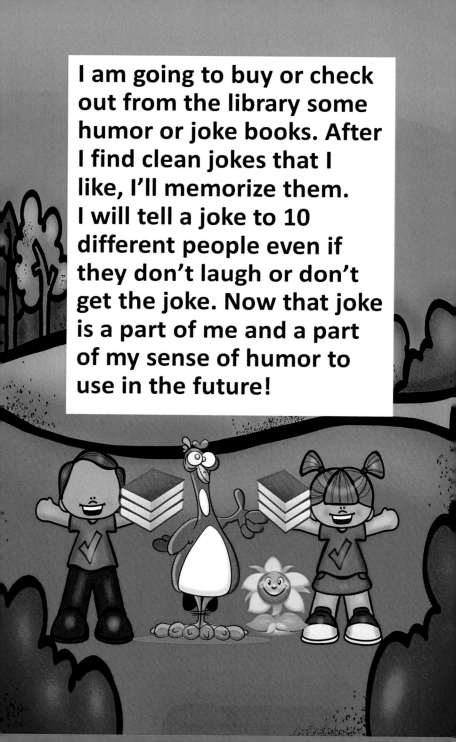

How to Tell Jokes

Do you know what you call a unicorn with two horns? The trick to telling any joke is a short pause before you tell the end of the joke. This is called the punchline which keeps your listener in suspense. Even if someone else knows this joke and says the punchline before you do, you can still smile, nod your head up and down or laugh with them. Anyone can learn to tell jokes. It just takes practice. If no one laughs at your jokes, that's okay since you need to learn from jokes that fail. Even professional joke tellers say that everyone doesn't always laugh at all of their jokes.

Practicing in front of a mirror with body language will make you better at telling jokes. Use your body language to tell a joke such as your smile, a finger to your lips, a head nod, a movement of your palm down to palm up, a shake of your head, a roll of your eyes upward, a shrug of your shoulder, and other body movements.

When your joke gets no laughs, you have to learn to read the body language of your audience. You can smile, try another joke or else be quiet, and later try your jokes with different people. Don't give up telling jokes. Learn from your mistakes. You can learn to be funny. Keep notes of jokes you like and memorize them. Study how other people tell jokes but try to have your own style.

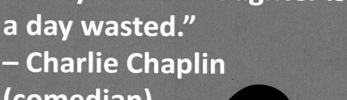

"A day without laughter is a day wasted."
– Charlie Chaplin (comedian)

Jokes are an important part of growing up. A day without laughter is a day wasted. If you have any comments, email me at richardvlinville@gmail.com Dedicated to my lovely wife Lastri, my grandchildren Mia and Kai, and to everyone who enjoys unicorn jokes.

Thank you for purchasing this book. The illustrations are from OpenClipArt plus Illustrations purchased from 1Everything Nice Designs and from Edu-Clips.com.

For over 40 years, I have enjoyed teaching at elementary, high school and college levels. I have written over 60 books for children, tweens, teens, and adults.